AUG   2017

Ada Lace

Sees Red

ALSO BY EMILY CALANDRELLI

Ada Lace, on the Case

Ada Lace

Sees Red

· AN ADA LACE ADVENTURE ·

REDWOOD CITY PUBLIC LIBRARY
REDWOOD CITY, CA

EMILY CALANDRELLI

WITH TAMSON WESTON

ILLUSTRATED BY RENÉE KURILLA

Simon & Schuster Books for Young Readers
New York   London   Toronto   Sydney   New Delhi

For the kid obsessing about grades. Don't worry.
You don't need to be good at everything to be great.
—E. C.

For Ava & Stella
—T. W.

For all the art teachers: The world needs you!
—R. K.

SIMON & SCHUSTER BOOKS FOR YOUNG READERS
An imprint of Simon & Schuster Children's Publishing Division
1230 Avenue of the Americas, New York, New York 10020
This book is a work of fiction. Any references to historical events, real people,
or real places are used fictitiously. Other names, characters, places,
and events are products of the author's imagination, and any resemblance to
actual events or places or persons, living or dead, is entirely coincidental.
Text copyright © 2017 by Emily Calandrelli
Illustrations copyright © 2017 by Renée Kurilla
All rights reserved, including the right of reproduction in whole or in part in any form.
SIMON & SCHUSTER BOOKS FOR YOUNG READERS
is a trademark of Simon & Schuster, Inc.
For information about special discounts for bulk purchases, please contact Simon &
Schuster Special Sales at 1-866-506-1949 or business@simonandschuster.com.
The Simon & Schuster Speakers Bureau can bring authors to your live event.
For more information or to book an event, contact the Simon & Schuster Speakers
Bureau at 1-866-248-3049 or visit our website at www.simonspeakers.com.
Also available in a Simon & Schuster Books for Young Readers paperback edition
Book design by Laurent Linn
The text for this book was set in Minister Std.
The illustrations for this book were rendered in Adobe Photoshop.
Manufactured in the United States of America | 0717 FFG
First Simon & Schuster Books for Young Readers hardcover edition August 2017
2 4 6 8 10 9 7 5 3 1
The Library of Congress has cataloged the paperback edition as follows:
Names: Calandrelli, Emily, author. | Weston, Tamson, author. | Kurilla, Renée, illustrator.
Title: Ada Lace sees red / Emily Calandrelli with Tamson Weston ;
illustrated by Renee Kurilla.
Description: First Simon & Schuster Books for Young Readers paperback edition. |
New York : Simon & Schuster Books for Young Readers, 2017. |
Series: An Ada Lace adventure ; Book 2 | Sequel to: Ada Lace, on the case
Identifiers: LCCN 2016053163| ISBN 9781481486026 (hardback) |
ISBN 9781481486019 (paperback) | ISBN 9781481486033 (eBook)
Subjects: | CYAC: Mystery and detective stories. | Science—Methodology—Fiction. |
Art—Fiction. | BISAC: JUVENILE FICTION / Readers / Chapter Books. | JUVENILE
FICTION / Science & Technology. | JUVENILE FICTION / Social Issues / Friendship.
Classification: LCC PZ7.1.C28 Ae 2017 | DDC [Fic]—dc23
LC record available at https://lccn.loc.gov/2016053163

Ada Lace

Sees Red

Chapter One
THE NEW ART TEACHER

Ada watched as her father returned Nina's picture to her. The assignment was a self-portrait in a favorite color. Nina had picked pink. Pink seemed like such an obvious girl color, Ada thought that Nina's choice might count against her. Ada's parents were big fans of going against "gender norms." If Elliott, her little brother, had done the same assignment in blue, Mr. Lace probably would have told him to "dig deeper."

To Ada's surprise, Mr. Lace smiled and said, "Really nice work, Nina. I love all the different tones you found in that color. You've reinvented pink!"

Nina beamed. "Thank you, Mr. Lace."

It seemed like he must be in a good mood.

Still, Ada was nervous. Maybe it was that her father had never sounded that excited about anything she had made in the past. The most she got was a "Good job, sweetie" and a pat on the head.

As he handed the other kids' pictures back, Ada listened to his praise. She tried to take it as a positive sign.

"Very nice contrast, Ethan. I can really see the details."

"I love what you've done with the ponytail, Pixie. Good texture."

"Look at those eyes, Casey. Brilliant!"

So, it was a surprise when Mr. Lace slowed near Ada's seat and placed her picture facedown in front of her. His mouth flattened into something that was almost a smile.

"Ada," he said. And nothing else.

Ada turned over her picture. There was a note that read *See me* next to a check mark.

Ada looked at her self-portrait. She had tried to draw a picture of herself—she really had. But it ended up looking like a sheepdog rather than a girl with floppy bangs. So instead she had drawn what was in her head: equations for Newton's second law, Einstein's mass-energy equation, and the Pythagorean theorem. She had thrown in some of her favorite constellations for good measure. The color she used wasn't like anyone else's, and she had added a little glitter to make certain details stand out. It had taken her a lot of time and effort, and she was pleased with the result. It revealed a side of her no one had seen before, which was, after all, one of the rules of the assignment. What could her dad—her art teacher—possibly have to talk to her about? She

could barely pay attention the rest of the class. They were drawing cubes, cylinders, and spheres. She drew the cube over and over again and never moved on to the other forms.

Nina ran up to her the second the bell rang.

"Gosh, your father is a good teacher. I'm having THE BEST TIME in his class. He's so encouraging!" said Nina.

"Heh, yeah! He's a real cheerleader," said Ada.

"I don't just mean the grade. The grade barely matters! I'm sure everyone got a check plus," said Nina.

"Right," said Ada. "Who wouldn't get a check plus?"

"He just knows what to say," said Nina. "I was so nervous about choosing pink. But it really is my favorite color. And it turned out it was fine! It's just what you *do* with it."

"Yeah," said Ada. "Nina, can I meet you at lunch? I have to talk to Mr. Lace."

"Sure. Hee-hee! It's so funny to hear you call him that."

Nina scooped up her stuff and bounced out of the classroom. Ada approached her father's desk.

"Hey, Adita," said Mr. Lace.

"If I have to call you Mr. Lace, Mr. Lace, I think you have to call me Ada."

"You got it, kiddo," said Mr. Lace. But clearly he didn't get it, Ada thought, because he just replaced one pet name for another.

"You said I should 'see you,' so I'm seeing you. See?"

"I do see," said Mr. Lace. He clasped his hands together.

"I know I'm not the best artist. I'm not like you and Mom. But I'm trying."

"I know, sweetheart. And your work was fine. But it wasn't exactly what I assigned, now, was it?"

"What do you mean?" Ada said. "That was my self-portrait."

"Heh! That's funny. It doesn't look like you!" Mr. Lace chuckled. "Are these spheres your ears?"

"It's my mind," said Ada. "I was being creative! Isn't that what you're supposed to do in art class?"

"Well, yes. But sometimes we need guidelines to really challenge our creativity. And the brown is a little dark. . . ."

"It's burnt umber!" said Ada. "What's wrong with it?"

"Nothing. It's unusual, but unusual is fine— great even! It's mostly that you didn't try to draw a picture of yourself. If you had at least tried to show us your face, or profile, or even your left eye, I wouldn't even mention the brown. . . ."

"Burnt umber," Ada mumbled.

Mr. Lace took a breath. He let it out his nose. Ada saw a little bit of dry snot pop out and settle just outside his nostril. She thought about telling him, but changed her mind.

"Okay, Ada. But the point is not the color. It's the assignment. I will always be your father, but now I'm your teacher, too. You can't just change the assignment as if this were an exercise we were doing together at home. Let me teach you. I give you guidelines to follow for a reason. Okay?"

"If you say so, Mr. Lace," said Ada.

"Good. I'll see you after school."

Chapter Two

COLOR ME ANNOYED

All day Ada tried to feel better. But by the time the last bell rang, she only felt worse. Her father said she hadn't followed the rules, but she couldn't help but think he just didn't like her work. Art wasn't Ada's favorite. When she had free time, she liked to do things like tinker with machines and observe ecosystems. It had never mattered much before that she wasn't an amazing artist. But now that her father was her art teacher, it suddenly seemed more important. She couldn't fail a class her father taught. That would be pretty sad.

She was so lost in her own grumpiness, Ada didn't wait for Nina or her father. She was almost out of the schoolyard when she heard Nina calling for her.

"Ada! Wait!" Nina caught up just as Ada was reaching the entrance. "Shouldn't we wait for your dad?"

"I guess," said Ada. They paused at the big

stone pillar next to the school's entrance. Nina hoisted herself up on it and then reached down to give Ada a hand. As Ada climbed up beside Nina, her burnt umber portrait fell from her bag and drifted lazily toward the ground.

"Oh! Is that your portrait?" Nina asked. "I'll get it!"

"No, leave it," Ada said. "It's not worth the effort."

"You didn't get check plus?"

"No. He said I didn't follow the rules."

Nina hopped down and picked up the portrait. She hopped back up and studied it.

"Heh. This is so you!" said Nina. "Even though your face isn't there, it's almost like I can see you in it."

"Thanks," said Ada. "But it doesn't have my face, so no check plus."

"Oh, Ada," said Nina. "It's no big deal. The plus barely means anything."

"Easy for you to say," said Ada. "Here he comes. Let's talk about something else."

"Okay. How's your robot coming?" asked Nina.

"Great!" said Ada. She loved talking about George. "I am working on his movement now.

Pretty soon he'll be able to change direction on his own."

"Whoa!"

As they walked home with Mr. Lace, Ada told Nina all about the different gears she was using and the programming language she was going to try out. She almost forgot her art class. But when Nina went inside her building, and Ada and her father walked home, Ada got annoyed all over again.

Chapter Three
Robot Rivals

Ada went straight up to her room and started working on George.

Before George, Ada had made a cart that could move Elliott's stuffed animals around, but it just went forward when turned on and had to be turned off to stop. She gave it to Elliott to keep. Then she had made something that looked like a bug and moved around by vibration. Elliott broke that one. Now she was ready to move on to something more sophisticated. Unfortunately, she had already run into a problem with the gears. She tried using a small gear and a large gear, but just couldn't generate enough power with her motor to turn the wheel and push the car along. She had replaced the gears with a worm drive yesterday. It was supposed to create more torque, or turning force. But now it didn't seem to be working for some reason. She couldn't get the wheels to turn.

"Hey, Adita." Her dad appeared in the door-way. "What's that you're working on?"

"My robot." Her dad was obviously trying to switch back to normal dad mode after being in teacher mode, but Ada wasn't ready to talk to him.

"Oh. How's it going?"

"Just trying to get these wheels to—"

"They're all locked up, huh. Can I see it for a second?"

"I don't know. . . ."

"Hey, I do all right with the stereo and the toilet."

But this isn't the stereo or the toilet, Ada wanted

to say. But she could tell her dad really wanted to help.

"Okay."

Mr. Lace took the robot and pressed on the front wheels.

"Maybe it just needs . . . a little more—"

"Dad, wait! Don't—"

"—elbow grease."

Ada's dad pushed a little harder on the wheel, and it snapped off, along with a piece of the axle.

"I'm sorry, kiddo," said Mr. Lace. "Maybe we can glue it?"

"No!" Ada was at the end of her rope. "That's okay. I'll go see Mr. Peebles. He'll know what to do." She gathered George's parts and left.

It was gloomy and overcast outside as Ada walked into the garden, and that suited her mood just fine. As luck would have it, Mr. Peebles was sitting outside reading *Gearhead Weekly*. His dog, Alan, jumped up to meet Ada. Ada and Nina had helped Mr. Peebles adopt Alan at the end of the summer. Alan wagged his way over and licked at Ada's knees.

"Hello, Alan. Good pup!" Ada scratched behind his ears.

"Ada!" said Mr. Peebles. "What brings you by?"

"Robot troubles."

"George not behaving himself?"

"I wish that were his problem! If I could just get him to move, then maybe he could get in some real trouble. That would be so much more interesting." Ada handed the pieces of her robot to Mr. Peebles.

"Uh-oh. It looks like he's been roughed up a bit."

"My dad was . . . helping me. At least he thought he was."

"Mmmm-hmmmm. No matter. I think I have just the parts. We'll get George fixed up in a jiffy." He ran upstairs to fetch his tools.

In less than twenty minutes Mr. Peebles had helped Ada change the axle and replace the worm gear.

"See, you can't turn the wheels with your hand. The worm drive has to turn them. That's why they seemed all locked up."

Ada placed George on the walkway and turned him loose. He zoomed away at full speed.

"Look at him go!" said Ada. "Thanks, Mr. Peebles!"

"You already had a great start, Ada," said Mr. Peebles. "You know, the Bay Area Robot Fair is coming up. You should see about entering George in the competition."

"Really? But he's still so rough. . . ."

"You have almost two weeks. You can get him there. I could help you, if you want."

"I would love that."

"Come to think of it, Milton Edison might be competing too. Maybe you can team up."

Ada couldn't imagine teaming up with a worse

partner. Milton had been a big pain ever since they'd met. He'd undermined Ada and Nina's investigation and tried his best to get them both in trouble. He'd probably booby-trap the robot to explode in her face.

But she did like the idea of competing against him.

Chapter Four
What's Fun about This?

The next morning Elliott bumped into the kitchen wearing a box over his head. It was painted with two big, round eyes and a rectangular mouth. A lightbulb stuck out of either side.

"MUST HAVE COOKIES FOR FUEL," he said in his best robot voice.

"Elliott?" said Ada.

"WHO IS ELLIOTT?" asked the robot replacement of Elliott. "I AM AMAZO. NOW GIVE ME COOKIES."

"Sorry, Amazo. The Laces don't eat cookies for breakfast," said Ms. Lace. "Here's a soft-boiled egg."

"Ew . . . I MEAN . . . AMAZO DOES NOT EAT EGGS. EGGS WILL JAM MY CIRCUITS."

"Ready, Ada-Beta?" asked Mr. Lace.

"Yup." Ada had almost forgotten she was mad
at her father, but not quite.

"Good luck with Amazo, Mom!" said Ada. "I'll see you tonight!"

"Have a great day," said Ms. Lace.

In science they were studying weather systems. Ada and Nina worked together to make a cloud using a plastic bottle, water, alcohol, and a bicycle pump. Ada had done it before, but it was still fun. Nina thought it must be magic, but Ada assured her it was, indeed, science.

"Clouds are just water vapor and dust particles combined with a drop in pressure. The altitude affects what shape they make."

"But *we're* making it using magic!" said Nina.

"Well, that and all this science stuff," said Ada.

In math they were finally moving on to order of operations. Again, Ada had done this on her own, but math was always comforting. The rules were well-defined. She either knew the answer or, when she did not, her mistake was clear and she could correct it easily.

In social studies they were talking about westward expansion. After that was art. It had been such a great morning, Ada felt like she could handle anything. She was wrong.

"Okay, class," Mr. Lace said. "We're going to work on something a little different, and hopefully a lot of fun, today."

The assignment sounded easy enough. They were to create something that looked like a striped sunset. Mr. Lace showed them how to mix the colors gradually, starting with a band of yellow in the middle.

"I add just a little bit of red to the yellow for the second band up—it's kind of yellow-orange.

As I gradually add more red to each new mixture, it becomes warmer, or more orange toward the top, until it becomes almost red. For the bottom of the painting you'll do the same, except using blue, so the color bands get cooler until you have blue-green at the bottom. Your color bands may not look just like your neighbors'. That's okay. Go ahead and start, and I'll come around to help."

Ada didn't really see how a color could be warm or cold—colors didn't have temperatures in degrees you could measure. She decided to just follow the rules as best she could.

The beginning was easy enough—Ada's band of yellow was perfectly straight. But when she tried to add red to the yellow, she must have added it too gradually, because she couldn't differentiate between the oranges. She tried to go back and add more, but it ended up looking like mud. She looked down the table she was sitting at. No one else seemed to be having any problems. In fact, she could see Nina making a second painting that worked diagonally. Mr. Lace walked around the room giving feedback to Ada's classmates.

"Good work, Ethan. Nice contrast. You might have made this band a little lighter, but overall it looks great. Casey, that's lovely. Oh! I like that orange, Pixie. It's so vivid I can taste it!"

Ada grew frantic. She couldn't stand the idea of messing up another art assignment. Sure, the idea of hot and cold colors was a little strange, but the steps seemed easy. She just had to add a little bit more red to each new stripe on one side, and a little more blue to each side on the other. It was a simple matter of proportions. So why did it look so wrong? She found a clear space on the palette she was using and tried to remix a lighter orange. But when she tried to apply it to the paper, she just got more mud.

"Beautiful job, Nina! On both of these!" said Mr. Lace. "The next step would be to do a round version, if you can imagine that."

"Oh my gosh, yes! Like the orb I see when I'm meditating!" said Nina.

"Sure!" said Mr. Lace, moving on to the next student.

Ada was not surprised that her friend had nailed the assignment, but did she have to nail it twice?

Mr. Lace was almost to Ada's seat. She desperately brushed on one more stripe. It didn't seem to help, so she grabbed a paper towel and tried to rub it off.

"Oh, Ada," said Mr. Lace. "We're having a little trouble here, I see."

Ada couldn't stand it. She looked up at the clock. There were eight minutes left before lunch, and she knew just what to do with them.

"Can I go to the bathroom, please?"

Chapter Five
ROBOT TRICKS

On the way home Nina talked excitedly with Mr. Lace about color and shape and all that other art stuff. Ada fell behind and tried not to hear. By the time they got to Nina's house, Mr. Lace and Nina had made plans for an art show.

"What do you think, Ada? Doesn't that sound like fun?" asked Nina.

"Sure." She really wanted to sound excited for Nina, but she just couldn't. And from the look on Nina's face, Nina knew it.

"Well, I'll see you tomorrow," Nina said, and hurried inside her building.

Ada and her father didn't speak most of the way home. He tried to make conversation, but Ada grunted in response. They had a rule about being father and daughter only inside the house and saving school business for in class or, maybe, on the way home. It was Mom's rule. She didn't want whatever was happening in class to affect their "father-daughter bond." So when Mr. Lace paused in the garden, Ada knew what was coming.

"Listen, Ada," he started.

"I'll do the rest of the assignment, Dad," Ada responded.

"I know you will, but if you want help—"

"Look, it's not a big deal. I just messed up. I can do it."

"Everyone knows how smart you are, Ada. But you don't have to be good at everything."

"I can do it, Pop."

"Okay."

Ada was tired of thinking about art, and looking at her father just reminded her of it. So she ran upstairs to find George.

"Well, hello, sir," she said to the robot. She turned him on and watched him roll back and forth. She connected the Arduino to a breadboard and then connected both to George, along with two sensors. Now George would have all the right stuff to roll across the floor and turn when he met a barrier. Ada fired up her computer.

"Now we have to make things a little more interesting."

Just then Elliott shuffled in, holding a deck of cards.

"PICK A CARD. ANY CARD."

"Not now, Elliott."

"THERE IS NO ELLIOTT. THERE IS ONLY AMAZO. AMAZO THE MAGIC ROBOT. PICK A CARD. ANY CARD."

"Not now. I'm busy."

"DOES NOT COMPUTE. PICK A CARD. ANY CARD."

"Fine!" said Ada. She picked a card.

"FIVE OF SPADES."

"Nope."

"Really?" said Elliott from inside the box. "That's impossible. Uh . . . THAT'S IMPOSSIBLE."

Ada held up the card. "Amazo needs reprogramming, I guess."

"AMAZO WILL BE BACK." He shuffled back out of the room.

Ada had only a few minutes before Amazo would come in with a new trick or her dad checked in about homework. She grabbed George and her dad's old laptop and snuck out and across the garden.

"Little Ms. Lace!" said Mr. Peebles, scratching behind Alan's ears. "What have you and George got for me today?"

"Well, I was hoping you could help me get started on his programming," said Ada.

"What did you have in mind?" said Mr. Peebles.

"Well, the contest says you should have the robot perform a task, right? So, I was thinking he could sort blocks."

"He could. You should know though, that's a popular task. If it's really done well, you might win some points. But you might want to think about solving a real problem. Give George a sense of purpose."

"Purpose," said Ada. "Okay. Like what kind of purpose?"

"Well," said Mr. Peebles. "It should help you

in some way. For instance, I built Rodney the robot dog because I wanted a companion like Marguerite."

As if on cue Ms. Reed came out of her apartment, and Marguerite barreled over and leapt at Alan. The two dogs twisted, rolled, and growled in a noisy little dog tumbleweed.

"Okay," said Ada. "I'll have to think about that."

"Maybe just keep it in the back of your mind," said Mr. Peebles. "The best ideas can take you by surprise. Anything else I can help with?"

"Oh, definitely," said Ada. "I have George connected to this computer, but I must have messed up the programming, because he's still crashing into stuff."

Ada opened up the laptop and showed her program to Mr. Peebles. After he'd read it over, he identified the problem.

"Read over these lines of code. Do you see anything?"

"Oh wow, yeah. There's a typo!"

"It's often just a typo."

Ada fixed the bug, and after a bit of trouble-shooting George was avoiding trash cans like a champ. It was a little harder for him to avoid the dogs, though. Since it was near dinnertime, Ada said good-bye to Mr. Peebles and headed home.

As she walked back toward her apartment, Ada saw Milton and his mother. Milton had a big blue shopping bag from Running in Circuits.

"Well, well, well. So that's your robot, eh, Lace?" Milton yelled. "You better teach it to fly if you want to win." Ada was too excited about George's progress to be bothered by her annoying neighbor.

"Talk is cheap, Edison!" she called, and headed inside.

Ada could hardly wait to tell her dad about George's new skills. He was always so interested in her projects. As soon as she saw him across the dinner table though, she could think of him only as her art teacher. Her disappointed art teacher. Even though they weren't supposed to talk about school, since Ada was thinking about it, she knew her father must be too.

"How's it going, Adita?" her father asked, passing her a bowl of peas.

"Oh, fine," said Ada.

"So you've made some progress since this afternoon?"

Ada knew he was talking about the art assignment, but she thought robots were better dinner conversation.

"Yeah. You should see all the things that George can do now. He stops at obstacles and moves in a perfect square."

"Well, that's good," said her father. Ada could tell he was working hard to follow the "no school talk" policy. Her mom stepped in.

"I think your father might be concerned about certain assignments you have to finish?" she said.

"Oh, that! Sure. I've got that covered."

"Do you want help? We can go through it together," said Ms. Lace.

"Nope. I'm good, Mom."

"Can I see your progress?"

"I want it to be a surprise."

Her father looked suspicious.

"It's due tomorrow, Ada," said Mr. Lace.

"No school talk, Pop!" said Ada. "Can I be excused so I can finish up my work?"

Chapter Six
INCOMPLETE

Ada cleared her plate and went up to her room. She lay down on her bed, picked up a book on robotics, and started reading about actuators. Then she put the book down and walked across the room and fiddled with a perpetual motion model. She took her turtles, Hydrogen and Oxygen, out of the tank and had them race for a baby carrot. She put them back in the tank and looked at the clock. It was 8:00. Technically, she was supposed to be brushing her teeth by now. She had wasted almost half an hour messing around. Why couldn't she just paint the sunset?! She had never had so much trouble finishing homework before.

She hung her failed attempt on her wall and

walked away from it. She stared at it for a good long time. The colors started to blur even more. Then she studied it up close. She turned it upside down. She hung it on the door. She hung it on the window. She hung upside down from her bed and looked at it again. Nothing seemed to make it better.

She took out a fresh piece of paper and her watercolors—a fancy set that her mother had gotten her for her birthday, when art was still kind of fun. She was never as good as her mom and dad or Nina, but she'd never worried about it. Her parents just encouraged her to play. Now that Mr. Lace was the art teacher, art seemed much more serious.

She laid her materials on the desk. Just as she had in class, Ada painted a band of yellow across the middle of the page. It was nice and straight. Then she added a little red to the yellow on her palette and made a second brushstroke across the page, just above the yellow band and touching it. So far, so good. She added a little more red to the mixture of red and yellow she already had. It didn't look that different, so she added more. Was it too much? She mixed a new batch

in another section of the palette with less red. She made a third brushstroke just over the second one. Was it redder than the second brushstroke? Was it the same? Orange-red? Or red-orange? Ada couldn't tell. She squirted out a new puddle of yellow and added blue instead. But the green she made didn't look that great either.

There was a knock on the door.

"What?!" Ada called.

"Whoa, easy there, tiger," said her mom. "It's just time for bed. Are you all done?"

"Oh. Sorry. Just about," said Ada. She sat in front of the desk so her mother couldn't see.

"Can I have a look?" Ms. Lace asked.

"No," said Ada.

"Ada. Love," said Ms. Lace.

"Mom," Ada sighed, "I don't want to show it to you. It's not good, but it will be done. I'll do a better job next time, okay?"

"Okay," said Ms. Lace. She looked at Ada for a long while. She ran her hand across Ada's forehead, as if to smooth out the worried lines. Then she kissed her on the top of the head. "It doesn't have to be perfect."

Ms. Lace backed out of the room and closed the door. Ada turned back to her paper and looked at the muddy stripes. She crumpled the paper up and threw it in the garbage.

The next day, all through science, math, and social studies, Ada tried to imagine how she could get her artwork done, but she didn't have the time or the materials. She really should've tried one more time last night.

Now it was time for art. The jig was up.

Mr. Lace introduced a new lesson and got the class started. Ada knew he must have expected her to turn her piece in by now. As he made his way to each student, the knot in Ada's stomach tightened. She was mad at herself for not finishing the assignment. She was mad at her father for having assigned it in the first place. And she was a little mad at Nina, too, for doing so well on it right away.

While Mr. Lace edged closer, Ada tried one more time to get the sunset pattern right. But something happened as soon as she painted that yellow band. She just couldn't bring herself to mix colors anymore. She felt as if she were color cursed. Why do it again if she were just going to mess it up? Besides, her father was only four seats away. She'd never finish in time. Instead, she labored over that one yellow band.

"Ada?" her father asked when he finally reached her chair. "Is this all you have of yesterday's assignment?"

"Well, in physics white really contains all colors, so technically . . ."

"I thought you said that you were going to surprise me," he said.

"Uh . . . surprise?"

"Ada." Mr. Lace lowered his voice. He always

lowered his voice when he was mad, which wasn't often. "I'm afraid you'll have to get an incomplete."

Casey Oliphant turned at the word "incomplete." Ada wanted to sink into the floor.

"If you can finish it by next Monday," said Mr. Lace, "I'll give you partial credit."

"Fine," said Ada.

She knew she sounded bratty. She felt bratty. But she didn't mean for what happened next to happen. She slammed her paintbrush down, and when she did, a yellow blob of paint flew across the table. It landed in a big splat right in the middle of Nina's new masterpiece.

"Oh no!" said Nina. "I was just about to put it up to dry!"

"Ada!" said Mr. Lace.

Ada felt awful.

"Why don't you go take some time to yourself, Ada," said Mr. Lace.

He didn't raise his voice, but that almost made it worse.

"I'm sorry, Nina. I really am. Your painting is still beautiful."

Ada couldn't look her in the eye. She went outside. But she couldn't bring herself to stop there, so she went all the way to the bathroom to hide.

Chapter Seven
THE BEAUTY OF BLACK AND WHITE

Black and white is underrated, Ada thought, examining the neat checkered pattern on the floor. The difference was so clear. It was easy to sort things that were black and white. Computers ran on binary code—0s and 1s—and black and white was the art version of that. Books were printed in black type on white paper, because it made them easier to read. If you wanted to say that two things were very different, you said they were like black and white. Lots of beautiful things came in black and white: yin-yang symbols, chessboards, panda bears. Why was it so important to create so many different shades of each color? It only confused things. She'd gotten better at drawing things in her field journal. Couldn't she just draw in pencil

or black ink? She wasn't ever going to be a pro-
fessional artist anyway. That much was clear. She
wasn't Nina.

"Ada?"

It was as if Nina had heard her thoughts. And if anyone could, it would be Nina. Ada almost didn't respond. Maybe she would just stay in the bathroom for the rest of the day and stare at the black and white tiles. Then she heard a humming noise and couldn't help but wonder what it was.

Ada opened the stall door. Nina stood there with her eyes closed making a loud, beelike buzz from the back of her throat. She opened her eyes.

"Oh! It worked! I was just willing you to walk out here," said Nina.

"I was wondering why my feet were itching," said Ada. "I'm surprised you want to talk to me."

"Don't be silly," said Nina.

"I ruined your painting!"

"No, you know what? It ended up being the best thing that could have happened. The yellow is almost exactly in the middle," said Nina. "The orb looks like it's glowing inside, which is exactly how I see it when I meditate! So, in a way, you fixed it."

"I'm glad I could help," said Ada. "It's probably my only victory in art so far. I must just be dumb when it comes to color."

"I can't imagine you being dumb about anything," said Nina. "I can help you with the sunset thingy, though. Do you want help?"

The truth was that Ada didn't want help. She wanted to be able to figure it out herself, but she had wasted so much time already.

"Okay," she said. "Thanks, Nina."

Chapter Eight
SOLVING THE GEORGE PROBLEM

Mr. Lace was not thrilled that Ada had disappeared after class. He called her out of lunch to chat.

"Ada. You're starting to worry me."

"Pop, I'm fine. Really."

"I just wish you would ask for help if you need it."

"I did! Nina's going to help me now." That wasn't exactly the truth, but it wasn't really a lie, either.

"Oh! Well, that's a great idea. But, listen: The assignment comes first, okay? Meet with Nina and then you can work on George."

"Okay."

• • •

Ada was going to go home, drop off her back-pack, and then go straight to Nina's to work on the assignment. But as soon as she saw George, she just couldn't resist him. Surely, she could just make a few tweaks before going to Nina's place.

The competitors were limited in the materials they could use to build the robots. Ada thought she could get George to feed her breakfast, but that turned out to be rather complicated. First, because it was difficult to define the task in code, and second, because George was having a hard time with the spoon. Ada thought that replacing his hands with a different kind of clamp would solve the problem, but that just created new problems. She wondered if George's new task was even going to work. She decided to run the idea past Mr. Peebles. She snuck George over to Mr. Peebles's stoop and showed him her different robot hand options.

"I can see the problem," said Mr. Peebles.

"Do I need some other kind of clamp?" asked Ada.

"It's always good to consider your options," said Mr. Peebles.

Ada sighed. She looked across the court-yard and saw Milton Edison ducking behind his curtain.

"Do you think there's a task that's better than feeding me cereal?"

"Better? I don't know. But there might be one that's just as good and maybe more useful to you. Have you gotten tired of feeding yourself cereal?"

"I guess not."

"Well?"

A few minutes later Milton walked past them, whistling. Ada stuck George behind her back.

"Hello, Milton," said Mr. Peebles. "Robot coming along nicely?"

"Yes, yes, yes indeed, Mr. Peebles," said Milton. "I'll let you get back to trying to save Ada's."

Ada scowled. She waited until Milton had left the courtyard before she spoke again.

"But if George doesn't feed me, what should he do?"

"I don't know, Ada. I'm not you. I don't know what you need help with."

"Right," said Ada. "It's my robot. I have to define the task."

"Think of him as a tool, not just a project," said Mr. Peebles. "It will probably come to you when you're thinking about something else."

But not thinking about George meant that she was forced to think about her art project. Nina was probably wondering where she was, anyway. Sure enough, just as Ada was leaving Mr. Peebles, she ran into Nina walking across the garden.

"Ada!" Nina called. "Did you forget?"

"How about tomorrow instead?"

"But why not now? Please? I've got all my best

supplies laid out: some paper choices, my favorite paints, some color swatches for reference and inspiration, and . . ."

"Okay, okay! I'll come over." Nina's excitement for art was almost catching . . . almost.

Nina's room was as unlike Ada's as it could be. There were so many decorations and frills. But somehow it wasn't at all messy—just complicated. All kinds of whirligigs and mobiles hung from Nina's ceiling—most of which Nina had made herself. A few prints hung from the wall—Matisse, Mondrian, and van Gogh. Ada recognized them from her parents' big art books at home. Nina's bedspread was like a field of flowers, and at the foot of it was a quilt. Ada guessed that Nina had made it herself. There was so much going on in that little space, it was overwhelming.

Ada wondered if this was what it was like to be inside Nina's brain.

Nina held up three pieces of paper.

"Which one would you prefer? This one's a

little thinner, but it's a nice, basic shade of white. This one is deliciously thick and creamy, but the white is more yellow. And this one is kind of in between. It's got a really good tooth to it."

Ugh, Ada thought. *Even paper isn't safe anymore.*

"You pick," she said. Every decision for this assignment was beyond her.

"Okay. Let's use the basic white one. I just start with yellow," she said, showing Ada the paint on her brush. She dragged the brush across the page, creating the first middle band of yellow.

"Then I take about this much yellow"—she showed Ada the pea-sized dab on her palette—"and I add . . . this much red. And I end up with yellow-orange." She dabbed her brush in the paint and dragged it across the page.

"With each new band I add a little more red to the color of the last band. As it gets more orange and you use up the paint, you don't have to add as much red to make the color change."

"If you say so," Ada said, "Queen of Arts."

Ada dropped some yellow onto an empty spot in her palette.

Ada watched Nina paint a third band above the band of yellow, but it was still hard for her to tell the difference between the second band and the third band. Nina continued until the top half of the page was filled with a bunch of stripes. Some of the stripes looked almost exactly the same to Ada, but she was afraid to say so.

"See! Not so hard. It's just like any other problem, Ada," Nina said. "You just have to break it down into steps."

Ada was just about to add her first band of orange, but she stopped dead.

"You're so right, Nina! It's a problem. And I need to solve it."

"Right!" said Nina. "Oh my gosh. I knew you would love this. You just needed the right tools!"

"Exactly!" said Ada.

"A good piece of paper, a palette—"

"And a robot."

"Wait. What?"

"Nina, thank you. I think I know what to do now."

"You don't want to stay and finish?"

"I just realized . . . I have to go home!" Ada ran from the room. "I'll call you!"

Chapter Nine
THE ART OF ROBOTS

On the way home Ada stopped at Mr. Peebles's stoop.

"Mr. Peebles! Colors!"

"Come again?"

"The problem is colors. George's problem. Or, my problem. George is the solution!"

"I see. Well, tell me more."

Ada explained her art assignment to Mr. Peebles and how she was having so much trouble with it. They talked about how a photoresistor could be used on a robot to detect colors. Different colors reflect different amounts of light. The photoresistor collects the light reflected from different objects and translates colors into numbers, which was a language both Ada and

George knew well! If Ada fitted George with a photoresistor and a paintbrush or two, he could complete her assignment for her.

Ada spent most of the weekend in her room tinkering and refining. Her parents had to call her repeatedly to come to the table for meals. Elliott came into her room at least twenty times.

"IS THIS YOUR CARD? AMAZO IS MAGIC! IS THAT A QUARTER BEHIND YOUR EAR?"

After Amazo's twenty-first trick, Ada locked him out.

"THIS IS AN OUTRAGE," said Amazo. "AMAZO HAS FULL ACCESS TO ALL ROOMS. AMAZO WILL BREAK DOWN THE DOOR. . . ."

Finally, Ada's mom noticed Amazo freaking out and recommended that Ada go outside "for some vitamin D." That was just as well. She took George for a test run outside.

Just as she stepped outside, Milton happened by.

"Nice hunk o' junk, Lace," said Milton. "If all the competition looks like your robot, this should be a piece o' cake."

He petted his own robot. It stood to his shoulder and looked like what anyone might imagine a robot would look like. It had a body shaped like a cylinder with a domed head on top, two LED lights for eyes, and a chrome grille where a mouth might be. It flashed in the sunlight. Ada was proud of George, but she had to admit he looked rough next to Milton's slick masterpiece. She had thought she would easily beat Milton, but now she had doubts.

"Let's see what that flashy thing's got, then," said Ada. She tried to sound more confident than she was.

"Oh no. I'm not giving away my secrets to the competition," said Milton. He scooped up his flashy friend and headed toward home.

Ada spent the rest of Saturday and most of Sunday aligning George's photoresistors so that they could catch the light, and debugging the code. Just before dinner on Sunday Ada's mom came in to check on her.

"Ada," she said. Her tone made Ada instantly nervous. "Can I see your art assignment?"

"Uh . . . it's not quite ready."

"I thought you finished it at Nina's?"

"Well, I almost did, but I didn't like it, so I started over."

"Your father has been patient."

"Mom, it's almost done. I promise!"

"But all I see are robot parts!"

"No, look! I've got the paints out on my desk. It's the very next test . . . uh . . . task. Really."

"If you don't have it in by tomorrow, you can forget about the competition."

"But, Mom!"

"I mean it, Ada."

Ada had been so sure George was ready to paint, but now the stakes were much higher. Getting a bad art grade was one thing, but she and George had come too far. She couldn't miss that competition.

"I will turn it in by tomorrow. I promise. Pinky swear."

They linked pinkies. Her mom gave her a kiss and left the room.

Ada turned George on. His lights flashed eagerly. She laid the paper, paints, and palette in front of George and attached a paintbrush to him.

"Okay, little buddy," she said. "Make me proud."

Chapter Ten

INTO THE SUNSET

Ada hadn't been so happy in weeks, despite staying up way too late to troubleshoot George. She was a little concerned that the stripes weren't as different from one another as they were supposed to be. But she had checked and rechecked the code, so now she just had to hope for the best.

She walked with her dad across Juniper Garden. On the way they ran into Milton, but not even his annoying smirk could darken her mood.

"Hello there, Milton," said Mr. Lace.

"Hello, hello, hello, Mr. Lace," said Milton. "Enjoying this lovely weather?"

"Uh, yes. Heh. Thanks, Milton. Ada, I have to run back and grab my planner," her dad said. He ran back toward the apartment. As soon as Mr. Lace was out of sight, Milton spoke.

"So, so, so, *Lace*. How's the monstrosity coming along?" he asked. "I hope you have all those extra messy wires tucked away."

"Don't you worry about George's wires, *Edison*."

"*George*? You're calling your robot *George*?"

"Yeah, that's right. After, George Devol, the *father* of modern robotics. Why? What are you calling your pile of bolts? Miltbot? Edisonic? The Miltonator?"

"No. It's Miltbot X6000."

"Ha!"

Ada's father came back down.

"We better hurry. We're late to pick up Nina," said Mr. Lace.

Ada followed him toward Nina's building.

"Later, Edison," she said.

"Wait, wait, wait! How did you know?" he yelled as they walked out toward the street.

"You're just that predictable, Milton!" Ada called back.

Ada had never looked forward to art so much. She was nervous, but excited. She had wanted to give her dad the assignment at breakfast, but she thought it would be better to wait until class. As soon as she walked into the art room, she pulled her art folder out and laid the assignment on his desk.

"Thank you, Ada," said Mr. Lace. "See. I knew you could do it. The style is unusual. It's interesting. Looks a little . . . robotic." He put the painting in a folder with all of the other student work.

After all her effort, Ada had really wanted
a much bigger reaction, but at least he didn't
say she'd messed it up again. She was just glad
she didn't have to try anymore. They had a new
assignment using cut paper. She spent the rest
of class halfheartedly working on it while she listened to her dad *ooooh* and *aaaahhhh* over her
classmates' work. He lingered especially long
over Nina's pieces.

"Very nice, Nina. The colors are so well-balanced, and I like what you've done with these transitions. Really brilliant!"

"Thanks, Mr. Lace! This one came to me in my dreams."

"Really?"

"Yes! See, I love to work in the morning, so every night I set up all my materials on the floor. Then I sit in the middle of them and meditate. In the morning I have art! The colors must ride in on my brain waves or something."

Ada snickered to herself.

"Huh," said Mr. Lace. "Well, it seems to do the trick. Keep up the good work!"

Let Nina have art. Ada built a *robot* who made art.

As Mr. Lace edged toward Ada's seat, she carefully hid her paper.

"Can I see what you have so far?" asked Mr. Lace.

"Oh, I have some work to do on it," said Ada.

"Just a peek?"

"I want it to be finished first."

"I can't let you hand in another late assignment, Ada."

"Don't worry, Mr. Lace! I've got this one covered. You'll have it by next art period, I promise."

Now that Ada had George, all her art problems were solved. Her *real* masterpiece was finished. She would let George do the rest.

Chapter Eleven
The Test

The next day Mr. Lace assigned pastels, and the day after that, prints with sponges, blocks, or potatoes. By just switching out a bit of hardware, Ada was able to have George complete each assignment. She managed to look busy in class, because she couldn't just sit and do nothing, but the real work was done by George. Ada didn't see any problem with this. Since she made George, and George made the art, she figured it was really her work anyway.

On Wednesday afternoon Ada was fitting George with his potatoes when Nina stopped by.

"I just passed Milton in the garden. Did you know his robot shoots sparks out of its head?"

"Oh really? That must be its newest trick. The

last time I saw it, it just had spinning lights."

"How's George?"

"George," said Ada, "is the BEST!"

"Oh! He has potato stamp hands! How interesting."

"You don't even know! Watch this."

Ada turned George on and let him do his thing. She had attached potato stamps, each with a flower shape, to his limbs. She had also set out several dishes, each with a different color of paint in it. George rolled over to the first dish and dipped his left potato in. He inched over to the second dish and dipped his right potato in that one. Then he made his way back to the paper and pressed each potato onto the paper. He repeated this process several times, until he had created a patchwork of bright flowers.

"Wow! He's quite the artist."

"I know! But those blues look the same. The photoresistor must not be sensitive enough."

"Which blues?"

Ada pointed to what she thought were two blue flowers.

"No. One of those is purple and the other is dark blue."

"Oh, purple. Purple's not really a color, anyway. Right? It's made up."

"What? Are you saying my second favorite color is a *lie*?!"

"Well . . . I mean . . . they're not that different, right? Just like this white pillowcase isn't that different from your white shirt."

"Uh, Ada?" said Nina. "My shirt is pink."

"It is?"

That's when Ada suspected her color curse might be worse than she thought.

Ada and Nina found a test for color blindness online. It showed a mass of dots of different shades. Ada printed it out and studied it.

"There's supposed to be a number hidden in there?" said Ada.

"There is a number in there," said Nina.

"Great. I can't see it."

"It's sixteen. It's shown in these green dots," said Nina. "See?"

"All those dots look the same to me."

The site where they found the test explained that Ada was missing crucial parts of her eyes that would have helped her tell red from green. They were called "cones." For a person like Ada, any color that had red in it could be a problem. As long as the colors were on their own, and fairly saturated, she could tell which was which. But when they were mixed with other colors or combined in a pattern with other colors, things got muddled. That's why she had problems telling the difference between purple and blue, orange and brown, and white and light pink. She wasn't cursed. She was color-blind.

"I must be adopted!" Ada said.

"Why?" asked Nina.

"How could two artists have a color-blind kid?!" said Ada.

"Well, you know more about genes than I do, but maybe it doesn't work that way."

"Yeah, and this article says that girls are practically *never* color-blind. So I'm a freak! I can never tell my parents," said Ada. "They'd probably send me off to live with my uncle Lucas or something."

"Are you kidding?" said Nina. "You're practically like a four-leaf clover. They have to keep you. It would be bad luck to send you away."

"That's comforting, I guess," said Ada.

That night in bed Ada stared at the ceiling for ages. If only Nina were right. If only Ada were lucky. Every time she imagined telling her parents, all she could picture was her dad's look of disappointment. She'd seen way too much of it lately. Now that she had George up and running and the competition to look forward to, she just wanted some time to feel like she was good at something.

The next day Ada handed in her flower print. For the first time her father looked impressed.

"Wow, Ada," he said. "Really nice work. The colors are nice and bright, and the shape of the flower is really pleasing."

"Thanks, Mr. Lace," she said.

"You got it, kiddo," he said. "I know it's been a struggle, but you made some real progress this week. You should feel proud."

Ada did feel proud for a second, but then she felt like a fraud. At least she was the one who had made the pleasing potato flower.

Chapter Twelve
Robot Style

After school Ada met Mr. Peebles in the garden to get his advice about enhancements for George. She was ahead of schedule and had time to add one more feature. Mr. Peebles was loaded with good advice. He gave Ada a little speaker for George, so he could make noises or even talk. He also gave her an old tin cigar box to house all of George's innards so he would look a little tidier.

As Ada walked across the garden toward her apartment, a flash of light near the fountain nearly blinded her. It was the Miltbot X6000. Sunlight blazed off its chrome like a roadside flare. Milton breathed on it and polished it with his shirtsleeve. He was trying to get Ada's attention . . . and on her nerves. She wasn't going to give him the satisfaction. She walked straight toward her door, whistling.

"In a hurry, Lace?" said Milton. Ada stopped before she reached the stoop.

"Milton. I didn't see you there," said Ada. "How's old Milk-Bone?"

"Funny. Hilarious. A regular laugh riot," said Milton. "Well, I'm sure you have to work on your pile of tin. I won't keep you."

"George has been done for days."

"But he's a long way from Miltbot standards."

"I'm not worried. Actions speak louder than chrome."

"Oh, don't you worry. Miltbot can act like nobody's business."

"Well, it's been nice trash-talking with you," said Ada. She walked through the apartment door and up the stairs.

Ada said she wasn't worried, and that was almost true. She was proud of George. He could do some really cool things. He was a better artist than she was! The problem was, she had spent so much time on making a robot that made pretty things, she hadn't made George very pretty. She wanted to believe the judges would score sub-stance over style, but George was all substance. He was in desperate need of some style. And Ada had an idea of whom she could get to help her.

That is, if that person weren't too busy helping Mr. Lace plan a school art exhibit.

When Ada got inside, she was surprised to find her mom in the kitchen. Ms. Lace was looking at pictures for the new exhibit at her gallery. Ada liked it when her mom worked at home. It was nice to see her in action.

"Guillermo thinks this piece is derivative, but it's one of my favorites," said Ada's mom.

"What's 'derivative'?"

"It's kind of like when an artist is a copycat."

The piece was all black, white, and gray, but the tones were so well-balanced that it didn't feel like there was any color missing. It was a large, close-up portrait from the nose to the forehead. The irises in the eyes reminded Ada of frost patterns. In fact, the whole portrait was composed of strange shapes. It was completely different up close than from far away.

"Ada? What do you think?"

"I love it," said Ada. "Those eyes are amazing."

"So, you think Guillermo's wrong?" asked Ms. Lace.

"Well, I don't know about the copycat part, but it looks cool," said Ada.

"I think so too!" said Ms. Lace. She kissed Ada on the cheek.

"Is Nina still here?" Ada asked.

"She's in the office talking to your dad," said Ms. Lace. "They've been talking about the art show, but I think she might just be waiting for you to come home."

"I don't want to interrupt," said Ada. "When she comes out, can you tell her I'm in my room? I need her help with George."

Ms. Lace looked at Ada over her glasses. Ada

was avoiding her father, and Ms. Lace knew it. But she didn't argue. Instead, she just sighed.

"Okay."

Just as Ada had finished packing all of George's wires, the breadboard, and the Arduino in the cigar box, Nina burst into her room.

"Nina Scarborough, at your service!"

"Nina! I need your expertise!"

"Oh, goody!"

"George needs some beautification."

"Hmmmm . . ." Nina took a long look at George. "I think I see what you mean. You know that Piet Mondrian picture I have on my wall? Well, that would look sooo amazing on George. It could really make him pop!"

Nina chose red, yellow, blue, white, and black lacquer paints. She outlined several boxes with thick black lines in an asymmetrical grid on George's torso and then filled in the boxes with the other colors.

"He's fabulous!" said Nina.

"You were right," said Ada. "It really suits him!"

After letting George dry for a bit, they arranged the photoresistors on the top of the freshly painted cigar box inside two foil cups so that they looked like eyes. Then Nina took the spotted scarf from around her neck and tied it around the top of the box. Ada pulled a little black beret from an old teddy bear and perched it over his eyes.

"There!" said Nina. "Doesn't he look chic?"

"So much better than Milton's pile of chrome and flashing lights," said Ada. "You're the best, Nina."

"Oh, you!" said Nina, waving Ada's compliment off. "I just know how to put together an outfit, that's all."

"And even I can appreciate the color scheme!" said Ada. "Every shade is in its place."

"Ada . . . have you told your parents yet?"

"No. But I will. I'm waiting for the right time."

Chapter Thirteen

ADA IS BLUE

On the afternoon of the robot competition Ada raced home. Her mother was in the kitchen answering e-mails. Ms. Lace had gotten Guillermo to watch the gallery so she would be free to help Ada. She had brought home two new tops for Ada to choose between.

"Are you nervous, sweet pea?" asked Ms. Lace.

"A little. But George is ready. We're both ready."

"Good. Why don't you try on the purple plaid shirt first. I think that's the winner. Call me when you have it on, and I'll have a look."

Ada found the two plaid shirts on her bed, but they looked almost exactly the same color. One

might have been a little lighter than the other, but they both looked blue. Then Ada realized why. She sat down and stared at her choices, not knowing what to do. If she put on the wrong one, her mother would know. After a while her mom came upstairs.

"Ada? What's happening? Why didn't you try the shirt on?"

"I . . ." Before she could stop herself, Ada

started to cry. "I don't know which one's purple! I think I'm color-blind."

"Oh, Ada," said Ms. Lace. "That explains some things. It's not a big deal. All you had to do is ask me!"

"I thought you would send me off to live with Uncle Lucas!"

"That wouldn't help—Uncle Lucas is color-blind too!"

"Ha!" Ada laughed through her tears.

"You know, some great artists are color-blind. Some people think Picasso was."

"I'm surprised he didn't end up with a purple period instead of a blue one."

Ms. Lace laughed.

"Anyway, I think we already know I'm no Picasso," said Ada.

"You don't have to be! You're one of the most

creative people I know. Look at that delightful
robot you made!"

"Thanks, Mom," said Ada. "I wish Pop agreed
with you."

"What makes you think he doesn't?"

"Well, he hates everything I make in class, for
one thing," said Ada.

"You know that's not true," said Ms. Lace. "You just have to follow the directions like everyone else. He's working extra hard to make sure that no one can say he's favoring you. He loves you, and he's always loved your projects."

"Then why isn't he here?" asked Ada. "Instead of with Nina."

"They will both meet us at the competition," said Ms. Lace. "Your father wouldn't miss it." She kissed Ada on the forehead. "This shirt is the purple one."

Chapter Fourteen
MAY THE BEST BLOCK SORTER WIN

Ada ended up wearing the blue shirt. It matched George better. The competition was at the Greater Bay Area Convention Center. Her mother drove them there, and Elliott came too. All the way to the convention center the robot replacement of Elliott pulled scarves out of the back of Ada's seat and tried, unsuccessfully, to turn water into confetti. Luckily, Ada's mom had a roll of paper towels handy. But then he really went too far.

"WATCH ME MAKE GEORGE DISAPPEAR," said Elliott.

"You do and I'll scrap you for parts, Amazo," said Ada.

"Mom!"

"Elliott, just leave your sister and George alone!" said Ms. Lace.

The center was big and echoey, and hummed with little groups making last-minute tweaks and strategizing. It was exciting and intimidating all at once. All of the "engineers" in the competition were twelve and under. Ada noticed that not all the robots were competition robots. One corner of the auditorium was an exposition area with flashy and artful new technology. Her instinct was to go find her father and drag him over there. Despite what her mother said, Ada worried he might not show up. Nina was so good at art, and her father really seemed to like being around his new students. Maybe he'd grown tired of Ada's techie ways. She didn't want to think about it now. She had work to do.

Ada looked around at the other competitors. Milton was there with his father, who was his mentor. Just as Ada was about to fill in her paperwork with her mom, Mr. Peebles walked in. Alan was tugging at his leash, yanking Mr. Peebles toward a chocolate Lab at the far end of the conference hall.

"How are you and George feeling about your prospects?" asked Mr. Peebles.

"It's hard to tell," said Ada. "We don't know what these other contraptions have up their sleeves."

"George's skills are pretty unique," said Mr. Peebles.

"Well, thanks, Mr. Peebles," said Ada. "I'm proud of George no matter what happens." She still secretly hoped to win. And she especially hoped to beat Milton Edison.

The robots had to pass two tests. First, they had two minutes to follow a path through a maze, without running into barriers. Then they had five minutes to complete their chosen task.

There were five robots competing. The first robot ran into a wall while trying to move through the maze and was eliminated. The next one completed the maze, but almost went over its time limit. Ada was feeling confident. George was up next.

George moved around the maze quite smoothly. When he met a barrier, he turned just as he was supposed to. When he had finished his patrol, he rolled back to Ada like a loyal pet. Ada was thrilled! Then it was Milton's turn.

Miltbot X6000 was more sophisticated than Ada wanted to admit. She saw him run full speed at the barrier and stop all at once. He finished the maze in half the time that George had.

Now it was time for the chosen task. Ada scanned the crowd. She saw her mom sitting next to Mr. Peebles, but her dad still had not shown up.

The first robot sorted wooden blocks into piles of large and small. Ada was relieved she had picked something different for George to do. The second robot pushed plastic blocks through a shape sorter. She looked at Mr. Peebles and smiled. He winked. Ada was feeling very good about her prospects. The judges awarded extra points for unusual tasks. She could have second place, at least. But, oh, how she would hate to lose to Milton. And she wished her father were here. It was George's turn.

She straightened George's beret, attached a paintbrush to him, and set up an easel and paints. She looked around the room one last time.

At the far corner of the conference room there was a flash of color and noise. It was Nina with Mr. Lace! They each shook a handmade pom-pom in the air. Ada's dad gave her a dramatic wink and a thumbs-up. Ada's mom had been right. He was there just in time.

Ada set George loose. He rolled over to the

paint and, hue by hue, completed Mr. Lace's first color band assignment. Ada had run him through this routine a few times in the past week and he'd gotten better and better at it. Now all the colors met neatly at the edges, so that there was no white space on the entire page.

The crowd went wild. Ada beamed with pride.

Now it was Milton's turn. Milton sat at a small, foldable table in the center of the exhibition area. There was a bowl, a spoon, and a box of cereal in front of him. Ada looked at Mr. Peebles again, who shrugged. Milton had stolen the idea for the feeding task that Ada had decided not to use.

Miltbot rolled in, holding a cloth napkin in one clamplike hand. His chrome dome glinted in the lights of the stadium, and his gears whirred happily. He tucked the corner of the napkin in Milton's shirt. Ada was nervous. Sure, most people didn't *need* a robot to feed them, but it sure looked cool. Miltbot poured some cereal into Milton's bowl. Then he poured milk over it. Finally, Miltbot picked up a big spoon. Ada realized that Milton had used a large serving spoon so that Miltbot would be able to hold it more easily. Smart. Miltbot scooped cereal out of the bowl and delivered it to Milton's mouth . . . almost. His targeting was off, and instead of making it all the way, Miltbot dumped the cereal down Milton's shirt. The next spoonful went over Milton's head. The crowd and the judges erupted into laughter. Milton was furious! Instead of turning the robot off though, he threw the rest of the bowl of cereal at the robot.

Miltbot rocked back and forth. Something inside his chest went *pop!* and smoke poured out. The room smelled like burning plastic.

One of the competitors leaned over and whispered to Ada, "Maybe it's lactose intolerant."

Milton's father ran over, along with one of the judges. They started to argue. Ada got a little closer and saw that the judge had removed a front panel. Underneath Miltbot's shiny exterior was the kit robot that could be purchased from Running in Circuits. Milton had cheated.

"Young man," said the judge, "I'm afraid you're disqualified."

Ada had won the competition.

After the award ceremony Ada dragged Nina over to the judges' table and up to one of the judges.

"This is my friend and partner, Nina," Ada said to the judge. "She was responsible for George's appearance. I know that was one of the scoring categories, so I thought maybe Nina could get a medal too?"

"Is she here on the entry form?" the judge asked, looking through a stack of paper.

"Well . . ."

"Oh, never mind, child. That was a spectacular-looking robot, and we have enough medals here."

The judge reached under the table. "You know, Ms. Lace," said the judge, "I have a brother who's color-blind. I'm sure he would find someone like George very helpful! Especially when he's choosing ties. Oh! The poor man."

"Believe me, I understand completely," said Ada.

"You've really created something special," said the judge. She handed Ada the medal.

"Thank you so much!" Ada took the medal and placed it over her friend's neck as they left the conference hall.

"Hooray for Team George!" Nina beamed. The girls half skipped, half ran to meet the rest of the Laces and Mr. Peebles.

"Now that, Ada Lace," said Mr. Peebles, "is one handsome robot. And with a sense of purpose, too. You should be very proud."

"Thank you, Mr. Peebles," said Ada. "You know, Nina came up with George's color scheme."

"I can see her flair," said Mr. Peebles.

As they walked toward the car, Mr. Lace put a hand on Ada's shoulder. They stopped walking as everyone else continued.

"Ada, I'm so proud of you," said Mr. Lace. "I wish I had known about your color blindness. We could have come up with other assignments for you."

"I figured out a way to finish them, didn't I?" said Ada.

"You did. And a very inventive way too. But don't you think it took more time than it would have with . . . human help?"

"Well, maybe," said Ada. "But I got George out of it! And, in a way, if I hadn't had so much trouble, George wouldn't be so good."

"That's a good way to look at it," said Mr. Lace. "But I would like to help you to do some art without a robot. That is, if you haven't made me obsolete."

"No way, Pop!" said Ada. "That could never happen."

Chapter Fifteen
THE ART SHOW

Ada brought George to the art show. He still had on a beret, but instead of the scarf around his neck, he wore his medal. Ada had finished a new set of enhancements the evening before and was eager to try them out. She went in ahead of her mother, who was still trying to wrangle Elliott inside.

Ada turned George on and let him roll along behind her. They entered the Cafetorium. Ada was impressed. It looked like an event that Ada's mother might have held at her gallery. Off to the side was a table full of teas, cookies, and punch. Nina greeted attendees with a stack of brochures. People could buy the artwork, and all the proceeds funded more art events and education.

George rolled by the artwork. His photo-resistors were trained on the easels above him. As he passed, he responded to each piece.

"Balanced. Nice contrast."

Nina met Ada and George as they were half-way down the first wall. She was wearing the medal that matched George's.

"Look, George," said Nina, holding up her medal. "We're twins!" George turned and fixed his sensors on Nina's medal.

"Brilliant," he said. Then he continued with the rest of the exhibit.

"Is he judging the artwork?" asked Nina.

"Sort of," said Ada. "He recognizes art in a limited way. If it has bright colors or a clear out-line, that makes it art to him. But what he says about it is just the words I put in his dictionary."

"That's really cool," said Nina. "I wonder

what he'll say about the center piece on the next wall."

"Why?"

As they approached the wall, Ada recognized that it was full of self-portraits. Nina's pink piece was one of the first ones she saw. But there, smack-dab in the center, was Ada's burnt umber drawing. It looked different. Nina had put a blue matte around it and framed it in gold. But not only that, she had created an overlay with a line drawing of Ada's face. Ada's head was turned slightly to the side, and all the equations, con-stellations, and shapes fit right inside it. Nina's changes fit in with Ada's work so well, it was almost as if they'd always been there.

"Where did you get that?" asked Ada.

"You just left it on the ground," said Nina. "It seemed like a shame to lose it."

"I can't believe it's mine," said Ada. "It's so much better now!"

"I just knew how to bring out its best qualities," said Nina.

George continued to bump along, cycling through adjectives.

"Brilliant. Balanced." He paused next to Ada. "Ooooooo," he said, his photoresistor fixed on Ada's portrait.

"Ha! That's a funny one," said Nina.

"That's weird," said Ada. "I don't remember including that in the language."

They reached the next wall, which had a few of the color studies from class. Ada recognized George's piece.

"Warm. Balanced," said George, passing quickly by the first few paintings. Then he rolled in front of his own. He stopped. The volume on his voice seemed to rise.

"DERIVATIVE! DERIVATIVE! DERIVA-TIVE!" he exclaimed. He rolled back and forth into the wall.

"Uh-oh," said Ada.

"An artist is always his own worst critic," said Nina, sadly.

"DERIVATIVE." George's lights flashed. It was the closest the robot could get to looking offended.

Ada's parents ran over. People turned and stared. One man searched his brochure.

"How much for the robot?" he asked. "It's really a brilliant piece. Wonderful commentary on contemporary criticism."

"Oh, he's not for sale," said Ada.

Ada quickly picked up George and moved him on to the next wall. He continued his critique.

"Where did George get his vocabulary, Ada?" asked Mr. Lace.

"He might have learned a little bit from you and Mom."

"I figured," said Mr. Lace.

"Maybe he can come fill in for me at the gallery sometime," said Ms. Lace.

George rotated toward Ms. Lace and scanned her with his photoresistors. "Derivative!" he said.

"Perfect," said Ms. Lace. "He's hired."

Behind the Science

GEARS AND ROBOTS

Gears are really great engineering tools. They're used in clocks, cars, and many toys. Depending on how you match them together, you can make things go faster, make things go slower but increase their force of movement, or change their direction of movement. I've used gears to create a miniature model of our solar system that I keep in my house! In my model, if you turn a crank, the Earth will move around the sun and our moon will move around the Earth. I created it all by using different types of gears. Ada was trying to find the right gear for her robotics project, and it turned out that a worm gear was exactly what the engineer ordered!

ARDUINO BOARDS

An Arduino board is like the brains of a robot. It's a little electronics board that you can connect all types of cool things to, like lights, speakers, sensors, and motors. Then you connect the Arduino board to your computer. Once it's connected, you can write computer programs to make your robot do different things. When you're finished programming, you disconnect the Arduino board from the computer. It will "remember" the computer programs you saved, and once you connect it to your own robot, you can bring your creation to life! Using a light sensor and LEDs, I've programmed an Arduino board to make colored lights flash when it senses that my room lights turn off. Arduino dance party! With an Arduino board, Ada can learn to build even cooler robots and gadgets.

The "Color" White

When Ada says that white really contains all colors, she's right . . . when we're talking about physics and light! Of course if Ada mixed all the paint colors in art together she would get black, but that's because paints contain pigment. If you mixed all the colors of *light* together, you'd actually get white!

Natural light, or "white" light, is light that contains all the colors in the rainbow. If you had three flashlights—one green, one red, and one blue—and you shined them on top of one another, you would get white light! Engineers use this concept to make your computer screens! If you looked at your computer screen through a magnifying glass, you'd see that the white areas were actually made of red, green, and blue pixels. That's just how humans see white light!

Want to prove to yourself that white light contains all the colors? Ask your science teacher to shine natural light through a prism. Different colored lights have different wavelengths, so each color will bounce off the prism just a little differently based on its wavelength and a rainbow will come out the other end! Who knew white light was so colorful?

PHOTORESISTORS

Photoresistors are a type of sensor that Ada can use to detect light. Photoresistors can tell a robot if it's light or dark in the room. Do you have streetlights in your town that automatically turn on when it gets dark out? Those streetlights are probably connected to photoresistors that tell them, "Hey, it's dark out. Time to turn on the light!" Photoresistors that are especially sensitive can measure the type of light they're seeing. A red apple will reflect a different wavelength of light from a yellow banana. A photoresistor can tell that difference and then tell a robot like George what color he's looking at!

Color Blindness

Most people who are color-blind inherited the trait genetically. Humans typically have three cone cells in their eyes: one for sensing red light, one for sensing green light, and one for sensing blue light. If you're color-blind, then one or more of your cones are missing or simply aren't working properly. About one in twelve boys and one in two hundred girls will have color blindness. So the fact that Ada is color-blind makes her pretty unique!

Robot Competitions

There are real-life robot competitions for students all over the country. When I was in high school, I competed in a robotics competition called FIRST Robotics. We worked all year to build a robot that would ultimately compete in a big arena against robots built by different schools. In order to win the game, each team's robot had to put its team's ball in a bucket at one end of the court. It was kind of like a robotic basketball game! Ada's competition was a little different from mine. Her contest presented an opportunity for Ada to show off both her technical skills and a little bit of her creative side! Who says art and technology can't go together?

ACKNOWLEDGMENTS

One of my favorite quotes is from someone I greatly admire, Bill Nye, who said, "Everyone you will ever meet knows something you don't."

The best quality someone can have is the ability to admit when they don't understand something. I've found that the people who admit ignorance are often the smartest people in the room. Never be afraid to raise your hand and ask the question. Chances are, other people in the room are just as confused as you are and will be grateful you did. The secret skill of a lifelong learner is getting really good at asking thoughtful questions to the right people.

I'm thankful for my friends Whitney L., Ally Y., Ingrid B., and Natalya B., who are always teaching me new things about science and technology. Surrounding myself with brilliant, bold women was probably the smartest thing I've ever done.

Thanks to Tamson, who taught me about the struggles of those with color blindness, a topic I was uneducated about before we created this book. Your words bring Ada's world to life and I'm so happy I get to work with you and Renée on such a fun project.

Of course the creation of Ada's world would not have been possible without the work and guidance from Jennifer Keene; my manager, Kyell Thomas; everyone else at Octagon; and Liz Kossnar. Thank you for everything you've done for Ada and me.

And finally, to everyone in my life—my parents, brother, husband, and coworkers—who aren't afraid to tell me when I'm wrong: thank you. You keep me honest during the times I should have admitted ignorance.